The Little Red Wolf

Amélie Fléchais

CUB
HOUSE

Freely inspired by the tale
LITTLE RED RIDING HOOD
by Charles Perrault

The Little Red Wolf

Amélie
Fléchais

CHAPTER I

Once upon a time, there was a family of wolves who lived in a deep and mysterious forest.

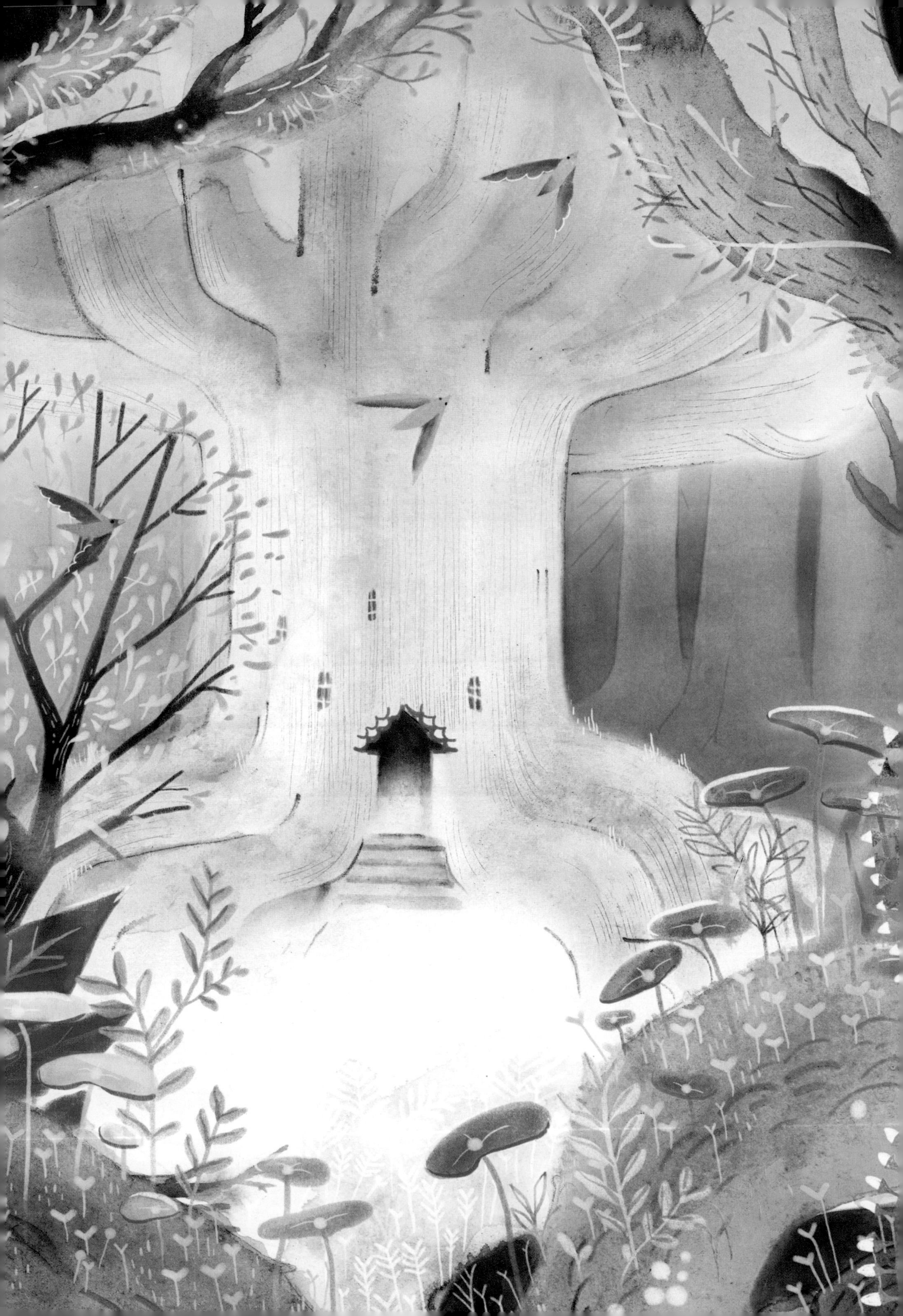

In this family there
lived a little wolf pup who
was always dressed in red.
Everyone called him the
"LITTLE RED WOLF."

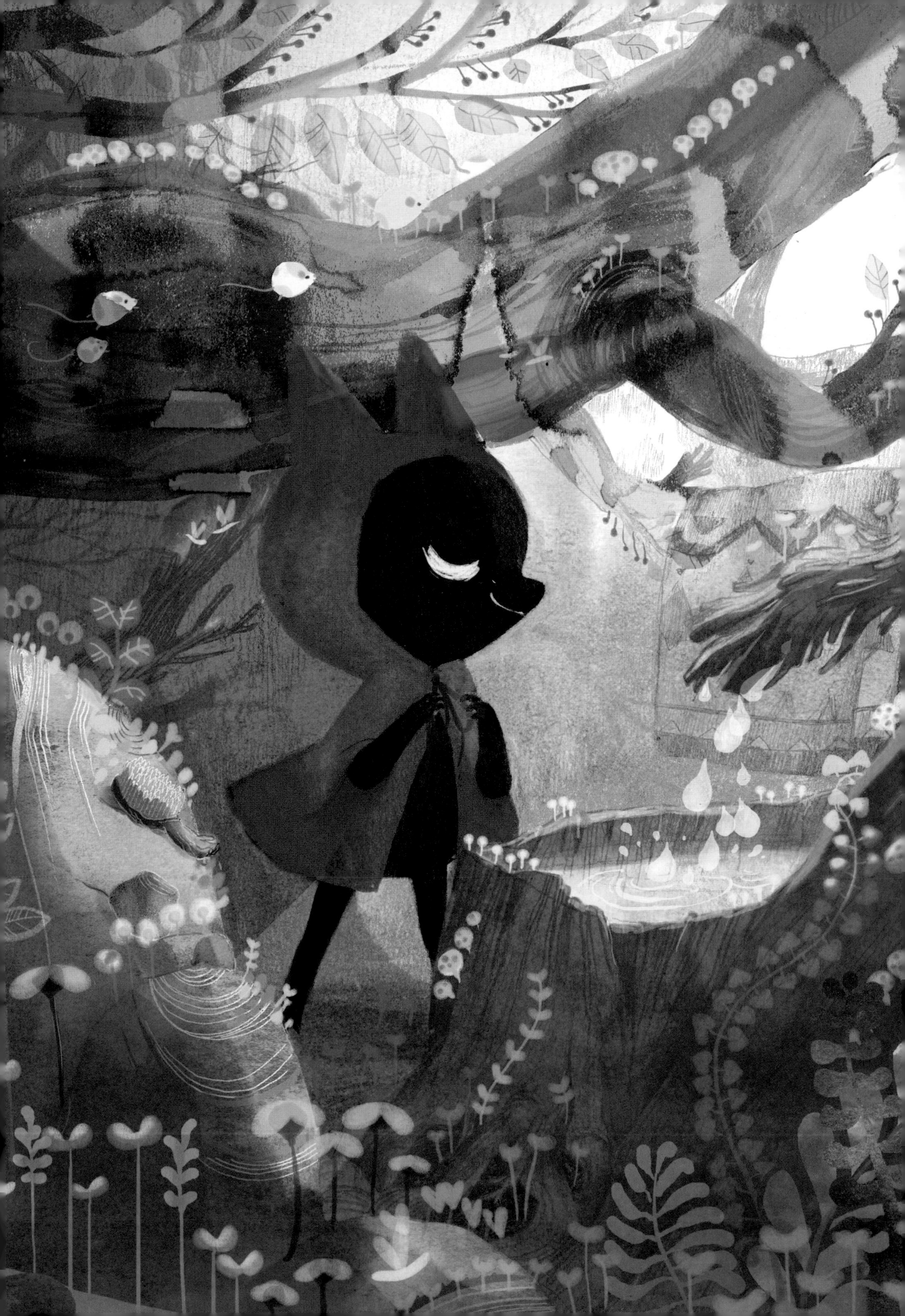

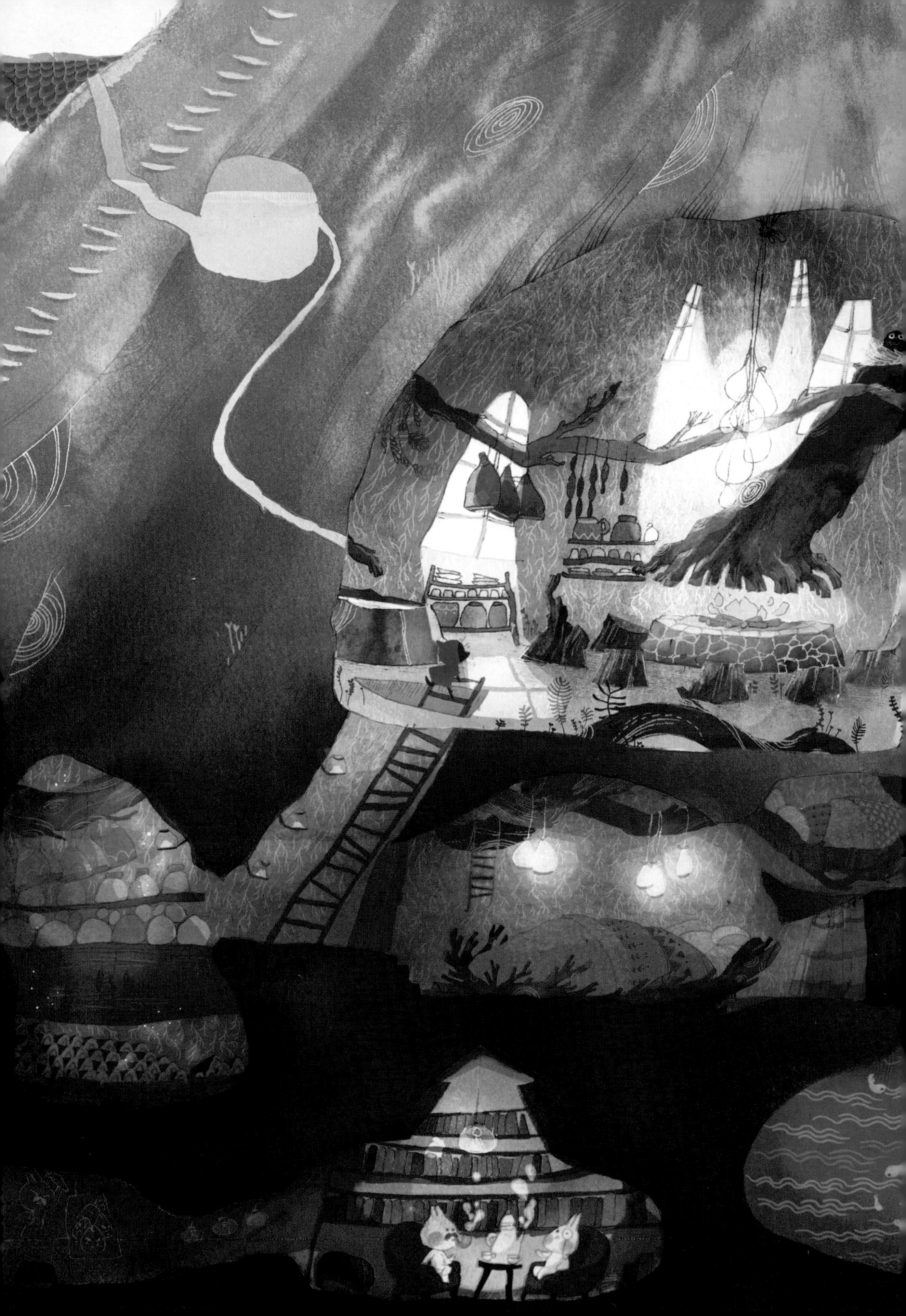

Sheltered by the roots of the forest's trees, the little wolf and his family led a quiet and peaceful life.

One day, his mother
returned from a hunt
bearing a few big
and juicy rabbits,
and told
him:

"Bring this
nice rabbit to your
grandmother wolf.
She's lost her last
teeth and can no
longer hunt."

The little wolf nodded as his
mother handed him the bundle.
She made sure to warn him,

"Be careful to avoid the forest of dead wood
where the hunter and his daughter live. They are vile
and cruel and hate wolves! I don't want anything bad to
happen to you, so make sure to stay away from there!"

The little wolf nodded a second time. He trembled as he imagined
monstrous humans with big, hooked fingers tearing little wolf pups apart with
their bare hands, and he promised himself that he would avoid that part of the forest.

And then he set off singing.

CHAPTER II

he little red wolf, already forgetting the danger, made his way through the forest without a care in the world, slowly straying farther and farther away from the trail.

First he followed a
little beetle...

And then he made his way
underground, following a bold
little mouse.

...And then he chased a gently
flowing cloud of pollen.

Exhausted by all the fun, he stopped for a moment.
It was then that he remembered his poor hungry
grandmother. He looked to his right, his left, ahead of
him, and behind him...the trail had disappeared!

But he was not at all worried.

"I am a wolf, the forest is my home, I'm sure I can find my way on my own, even without the dumb trail!" he thought.

And he set out once more.

What an arrogant little wolf!

Since he was a wolf, one of the strongest animals in the forest—as everyone knows—he let his sharp sense of smell and hearing guide him through the forest. But he soon grew tired, and his stomach began to growl, getting louder and louder.

"Hmm, grandmother wolf does not have sharp eyes. She won't notice if I eat one of the rabbit's feet!"

And with that, he promptly ate one of the rabbit's feet and continued on his way. But his stomach began to growl even more loudly...

"If I eat his other feet, she'll think the rabbit is so fat that his little feet are hidden under his stomach!"

And he ate the rest of the feet.
He continued on his way, except he felt hungry once more.

"If I eat his ears, she'll think it's a big mouse! Her nose is too tired for her to smell the difference."

Later:

"If I eat his head, she won't be mad at me. I'll leave her the stomach, the most tender piece. Besides, she doesn't have any teeth, she couldn't eat the head anyway!"

And so it continued until there was no more of the rabbit left. The little red wolf had eaten it all! Panicked, he looked at his bundle, which now only held bones.

At this time he also realized that the trees around him
all looked the same. He was truly lost and the rabbit was
gone. He was going to get in trouble, big trouble, for sure!
And so he sat down and began to cry.

CHAPTER III

The little red wolf cried large tears.

He couldn't stop thinking about his mom, his dad, his grandmother...they were all going to hate him! How could he fix this? He was in a terrible situation!

Suddenly, a soft voice called out to him:

"Why are you crying?"

The little red wolf looked up. A young blonde girl, dressed in strange clothes, was looking at him curiously. Surprised, the little wolf remembered that he had always been warned to "stay away from humans!" But this little human seemed so gentle, so small, that surely he could trust her.

"I'm lost," he cried, "and I ate the rabbit I was supposed to bring to my grandmother. Now, even if I find my way, I'll be in trouble..." He sniffed loudly.

The little girl, bouncing gently, answered in a kind voice:

"Oh, but I have plenty of rabbits at home! I can give you one, so you won't get in trouble."

The little red wolf was relieved. He stopped
crying and asked quietly:
"Really, you would do that?"
The little girl nodded.
"Of course, come with me!"
She took him by the hand, and the two set
off together.

The little wolf and the young girl walked for a long time.
The scenery changed, and the trees became thinner.

The young girl
hummed a soft tune.
Eventually, the little
wolf asked her:

"What are you humming?
It's very pretty!"

The young girl looked at him
strangely, and then said:

"It's a song that I made up, do
you want to hear the words?"

He nodded and the young girl
began to sing.

*"Once upon a time, there was a beautiful
young woman..."*

"*Who spent her time deep in the forest.*"

*"The people of the village
said she had no soul."*

"But the village guard
admired her deeply."

"And so they fell in love, and he
laid down his weapons..."
"And they lived a happy life,
deep in the trees."

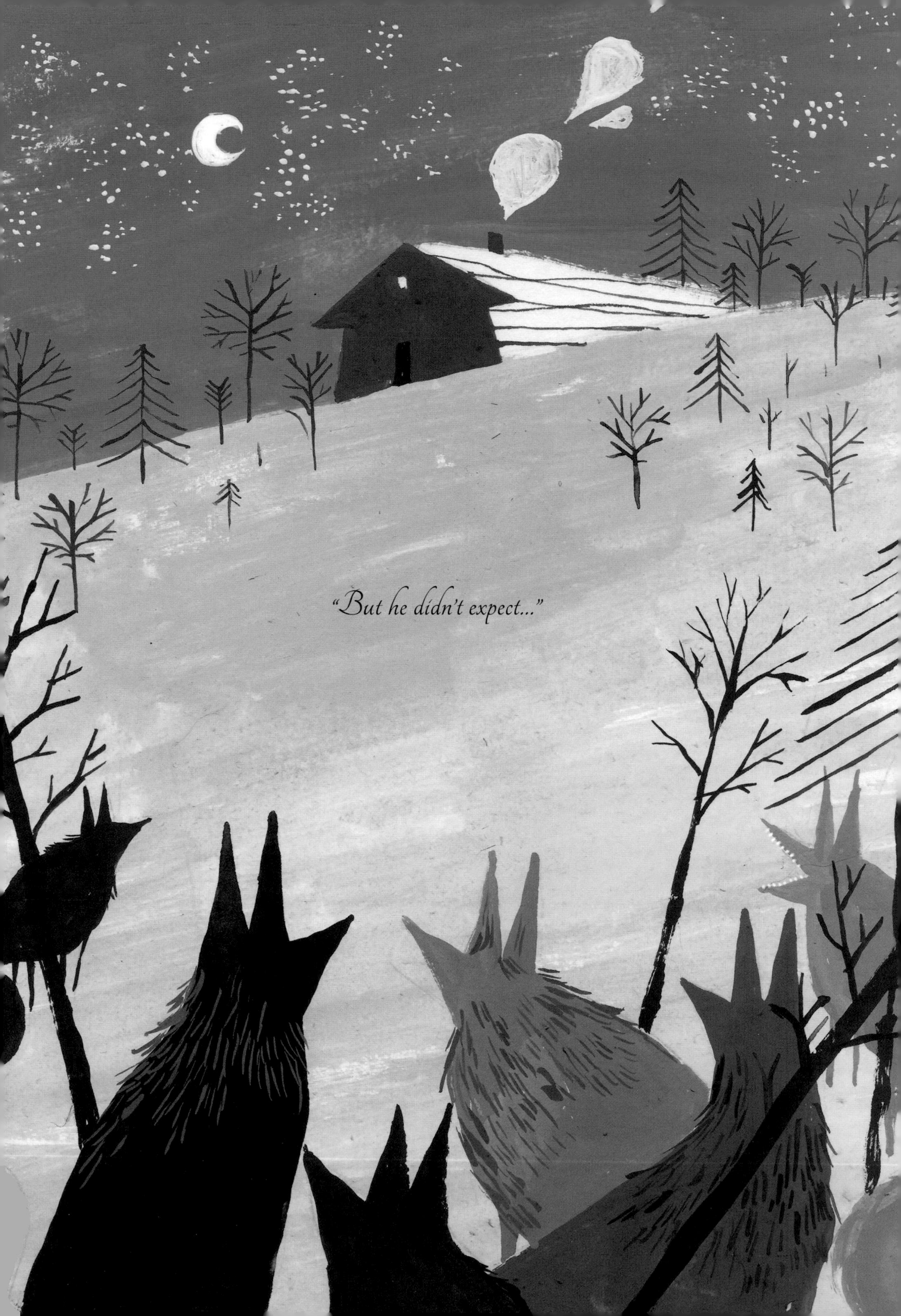

"But he didn't expect..."

Suddenly, the
young girl stopped.
"We're here. Look, I live in this tree!"

CHAPTER IV

he little wolf gazed into the clearing ahead of them...

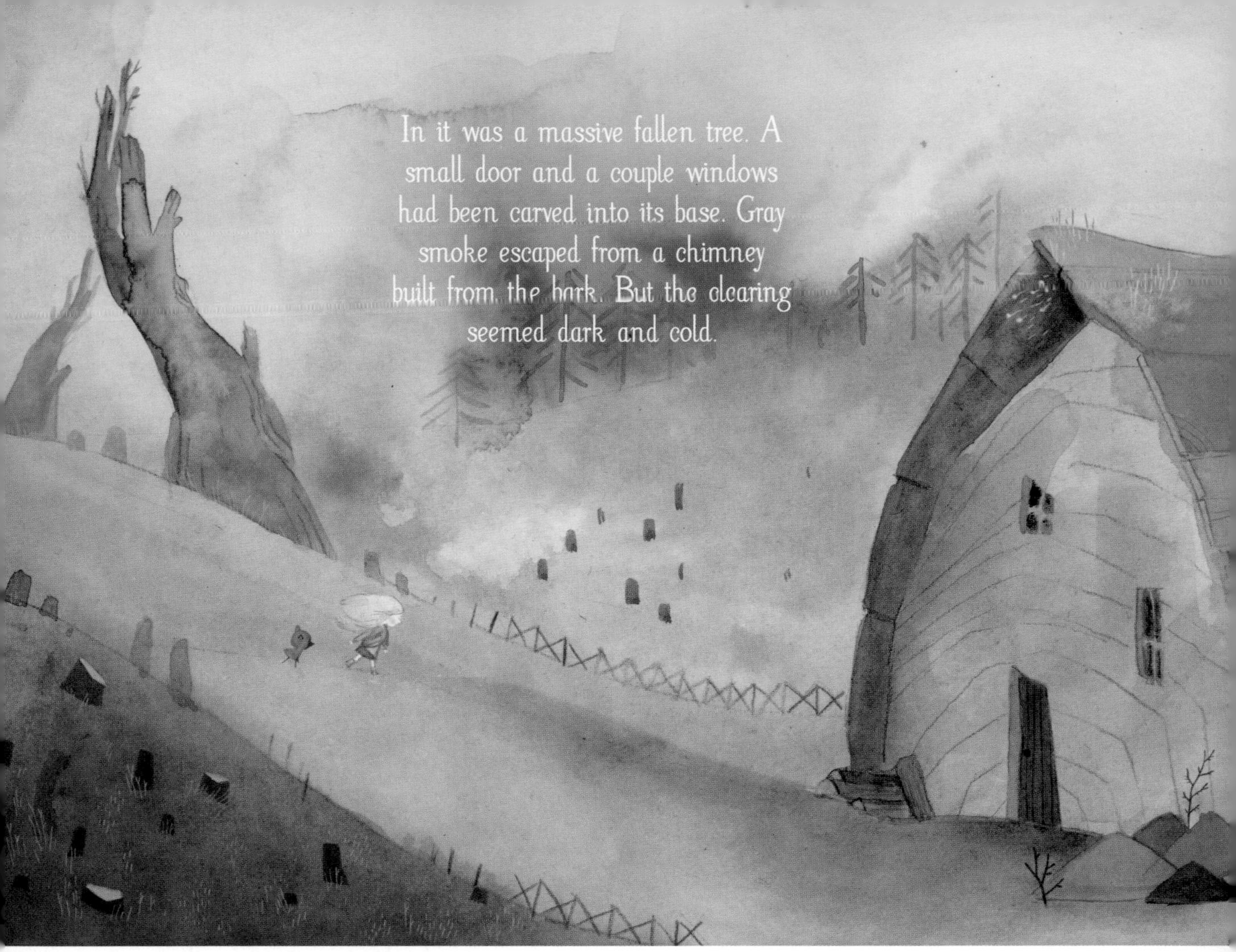
In it was a massive fallen tree. A small door and a couple windows had been carved into its base. Gray smoke escaped from a chimney built from the bark. But the clearing seemed dark and cold.

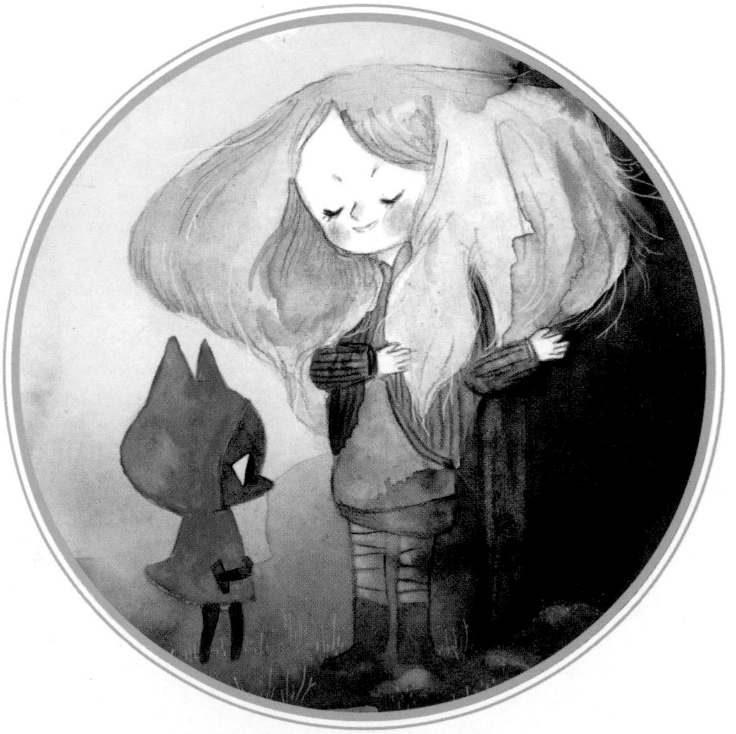

"Are you coming? The rabbits are inside!"

The little red wolf trembled, without knowing entirely why, but he listened to her and followed her into the somber home.

Just as he stepped inside, a horrible stench stung his nose. He walked forward, slowly, unable to see anything in the dark interior.

"Keep going! You're walking too slowly!" said the young girl.

"It's all the way at the end!"

Her voice grew harsher.

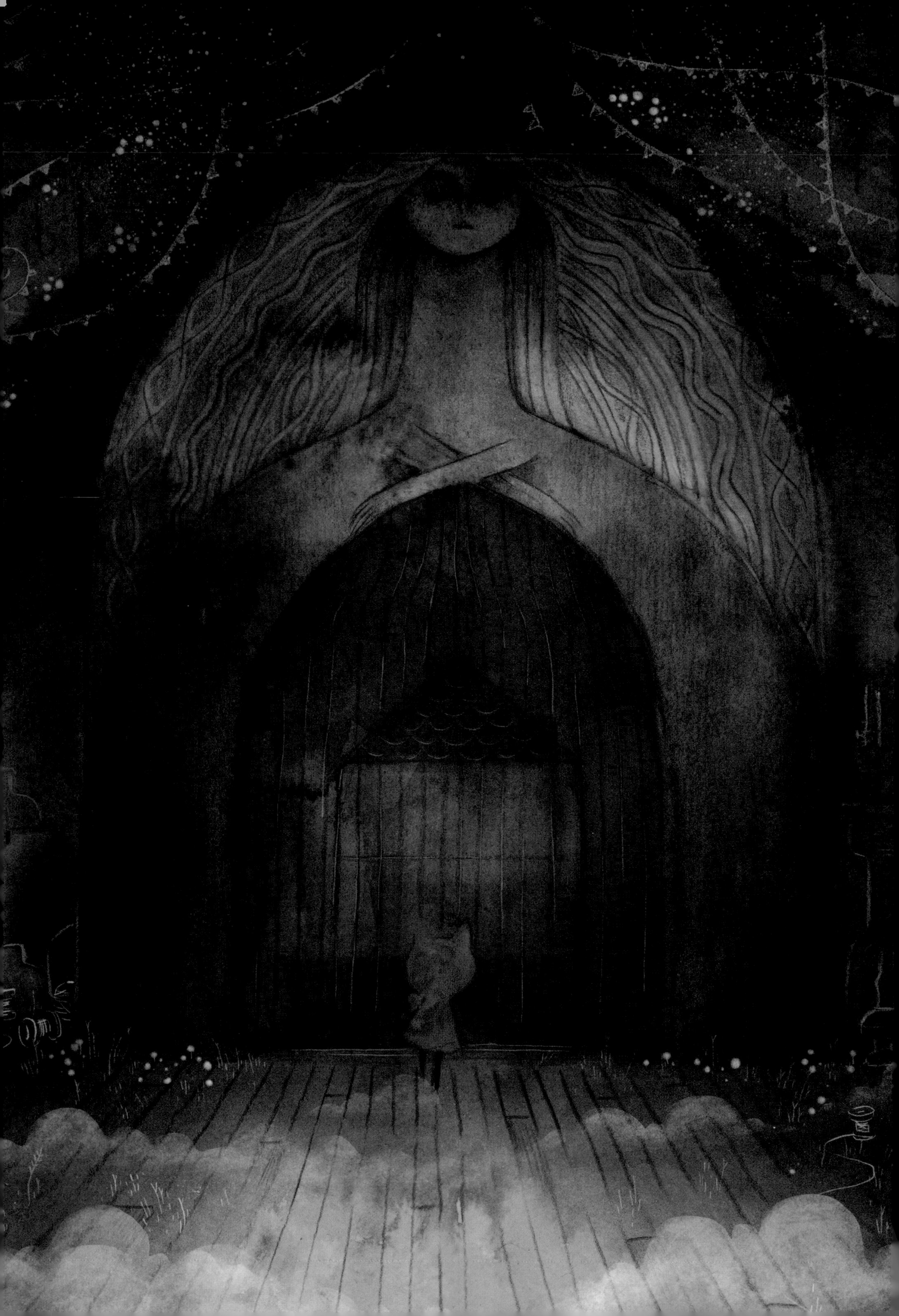

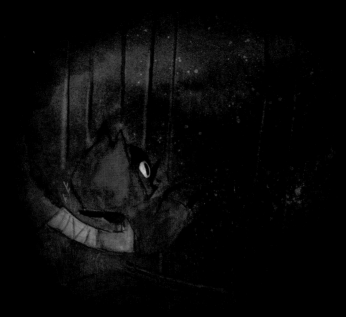

As his eyes got used to the dark, the little wolf could better
see his surroundings. But he barely had time to see the
strange cage in front of him, shaped like a large woman,
before he was pushed roughly inside and the door locked
behind him. He heard a little laugh.

It was the little girl, laughing and laughing. She laughed and she spun, and she even danced.
"Ha ha ha! My papa will be so happy! You wolves are so stupid!"
The little wolf didn't understand.

He stood up inside the cage and looked more closely at his surroundings. He was horrified to find wolfskins hanging from the ceiling, wolf heads mounted to the wall, and a rug of wolf fur resting on the ground!

He realized then: He was in the hunter's house and the pretty young girl that was dancing with joy as she made fun of him was none other than the hunter's horrible daughter! How right his mother had been to warn him! What a fool he was!

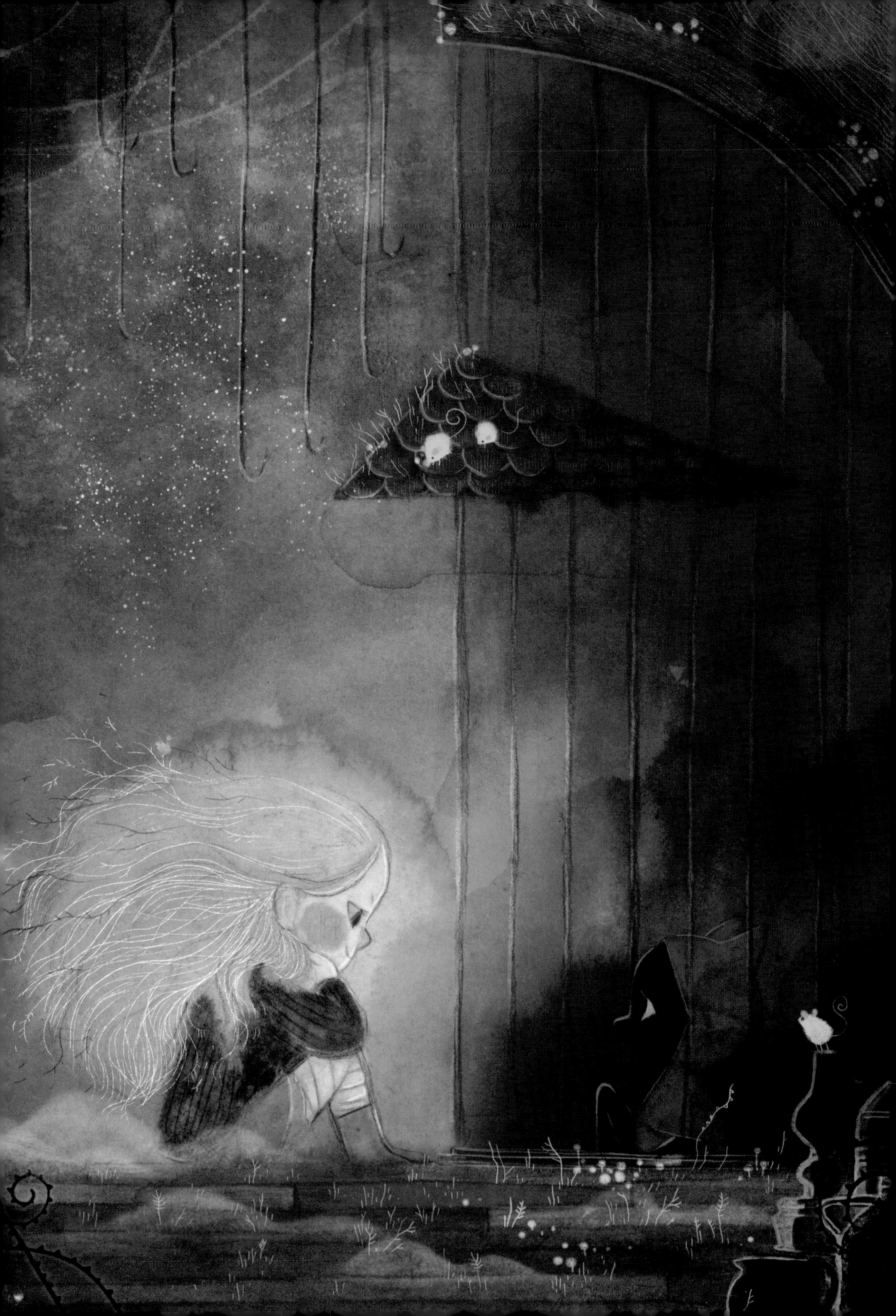

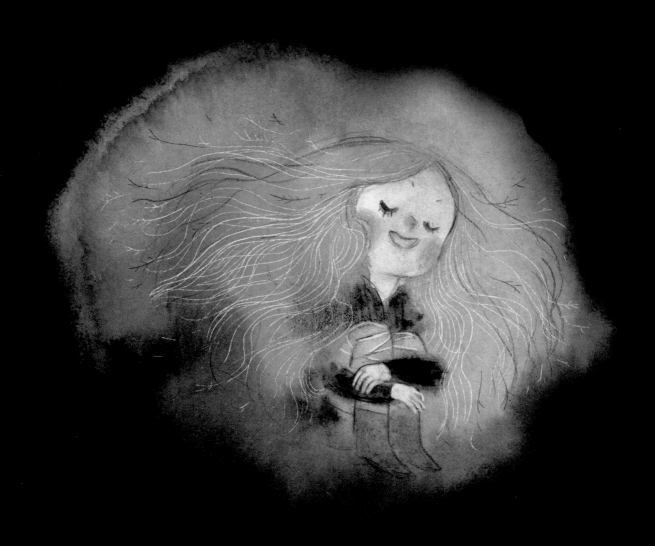

The young girl stopped dancing and sat on the ground, facing him, with a dreamy air about her.

"We have to wait for my papa now.
You'll see, he'll be so happy to see you!"

Then she continued her song...

"But he didn't expect
what would happen next..."

*"Because horrible beasts
were watching him."*

"In fear, the guard took
up his weapons again..."

"But misfortune came,
and he couldn't stop it."

"And ever since that day, we
kill the soulless beasts..."
"Because they all deserve...
to be erased..."

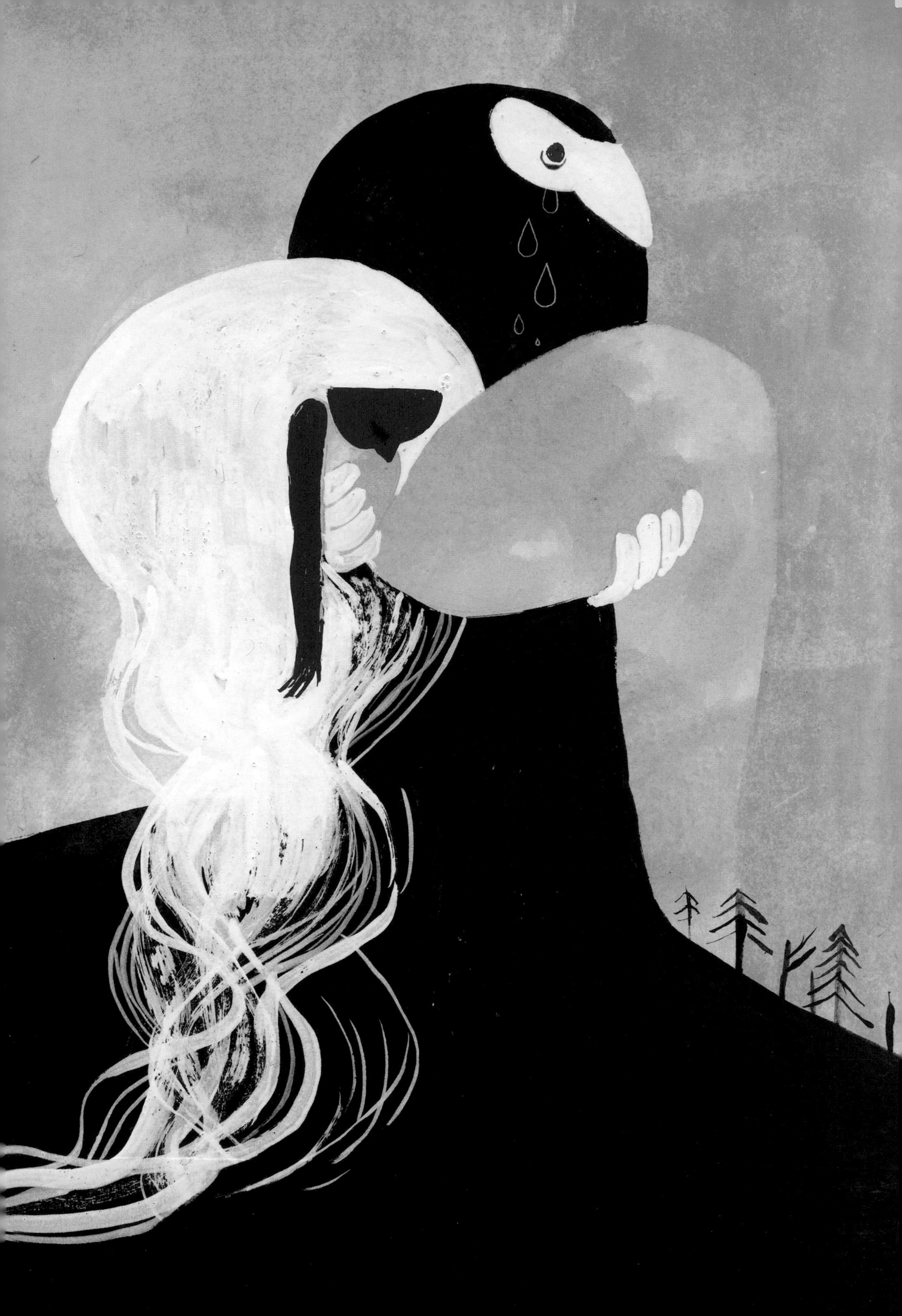

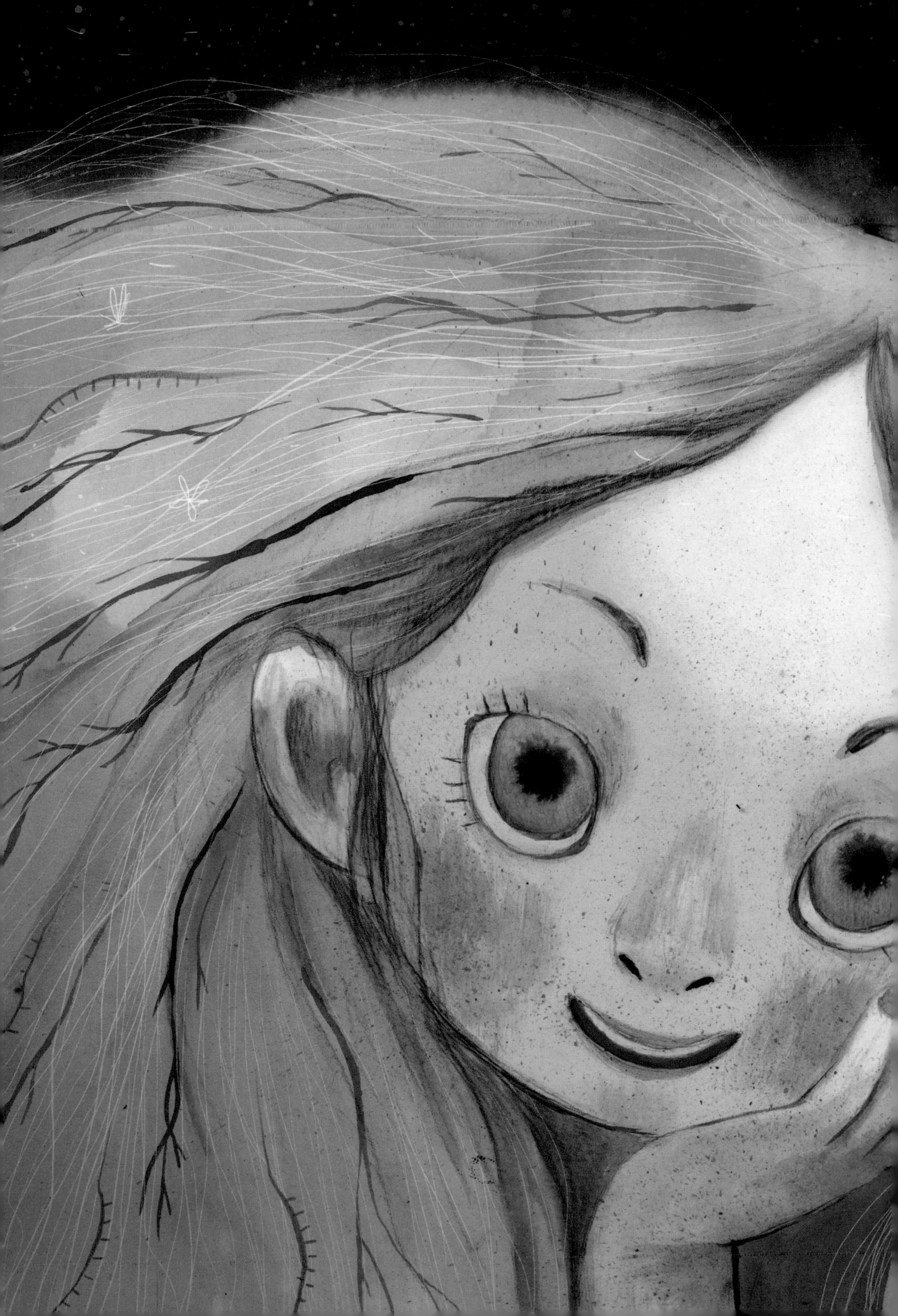

The young girl stopped singing.
"You see, you're all evil beasts. And that is why we need to kill you," she said as she neared the cage. "You only bring pain!"

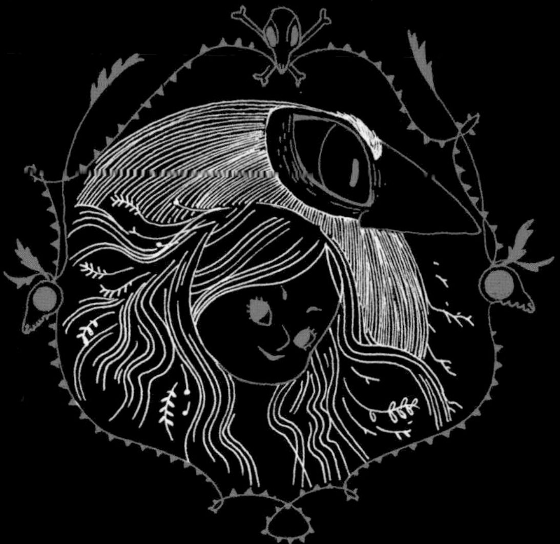

CHAPTER V

The door was shoved open, and light spilled briefly into the room before it was eclipsed by a dark, massive silhouette.

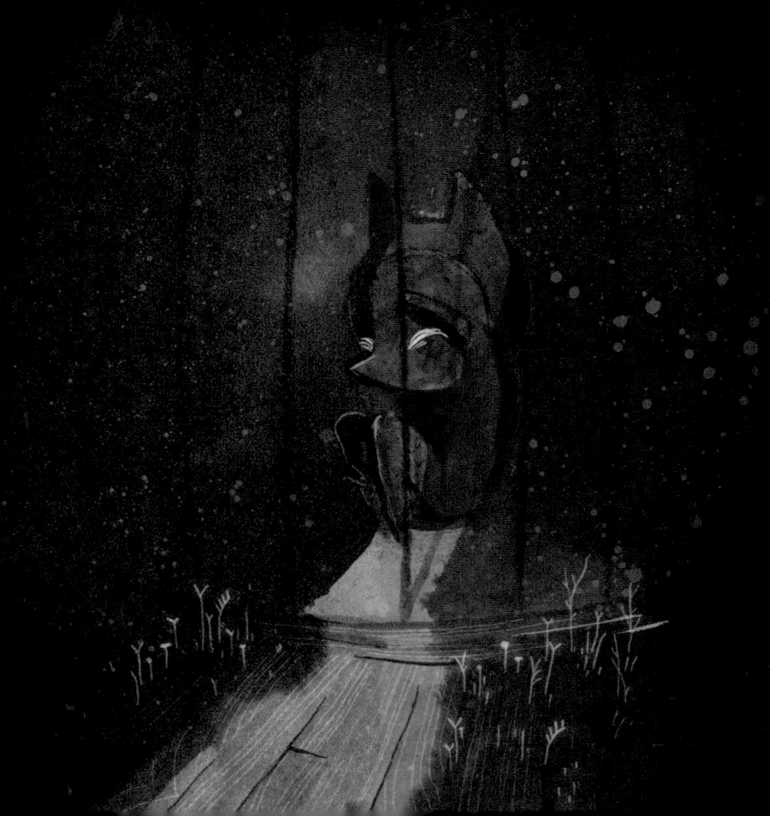

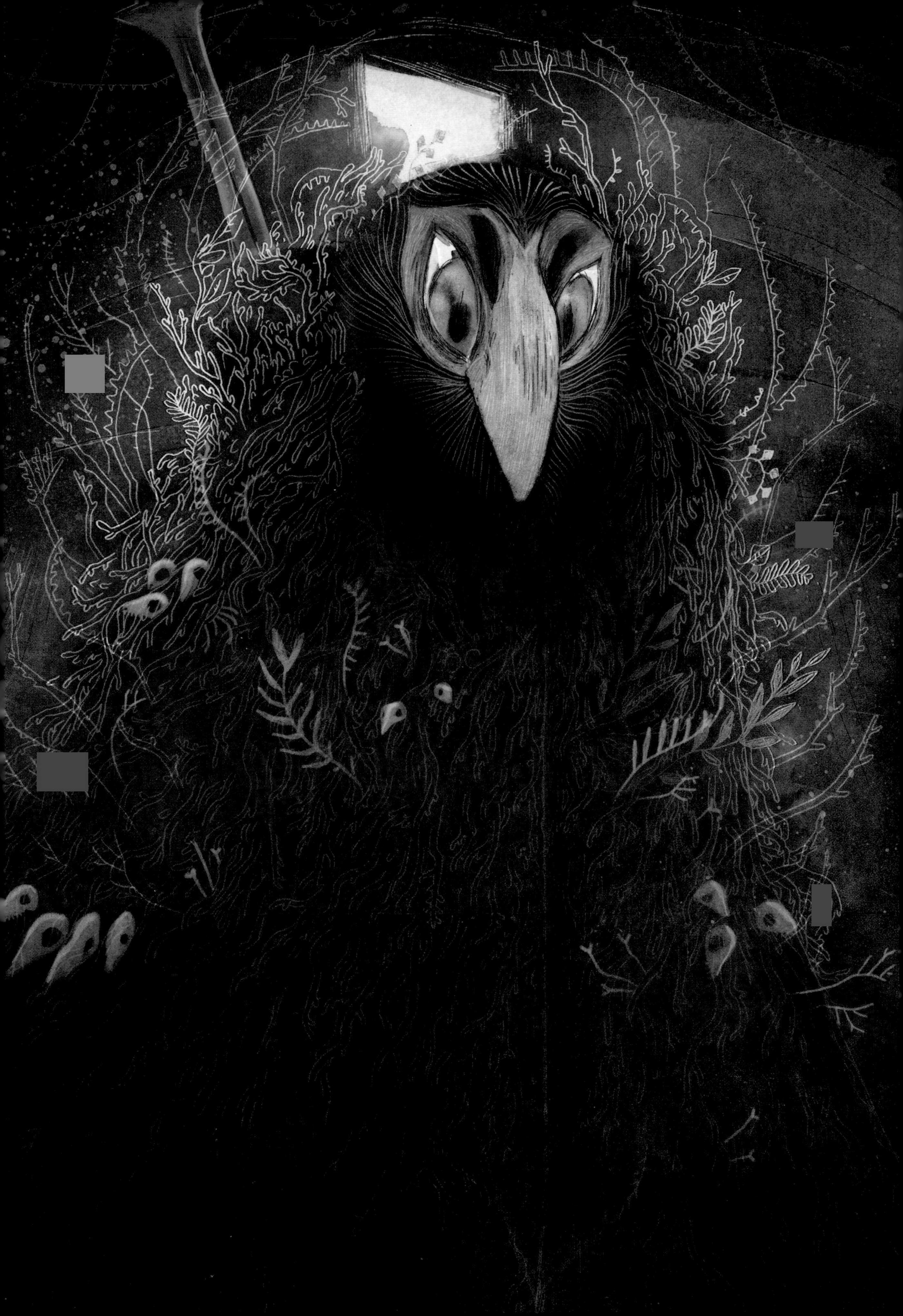

The little wolf thought at first it was his father, but when he took a better look he realized it was a human. The young girl threw herself into the man's arms.

"Look! Look! I caught one of the evil beasts!"

The man smiled and affectionately patted the girl's head.
"Well done, my girl. I'm proud of you."
The man approached the cage. The little wolf watched, worried.
This man had the eyes of a wild beast!

The little red wolf curled up inside the cage and screamed in terror. The hunter aimed his dreadful rifle at the little wolf.

The little wolf, petrified, covered his eyes. A shot sounded, and then nothing.

He opened his eyes and barely had the time to see a large cloth thrown over his cage before he found himself in darkness once more.

He heard footsteps, loud voices, a deafening sound.

Only a few minutes passed, but it felt like an eternity to the little red wolf.

Finally, the covering was pulled away. The hunter
and his daughter were tied up in a corner of the
room. His father was looking at him. He put on
his jacket, which had covered the cage a moment
ago, and took his pup into his arms.

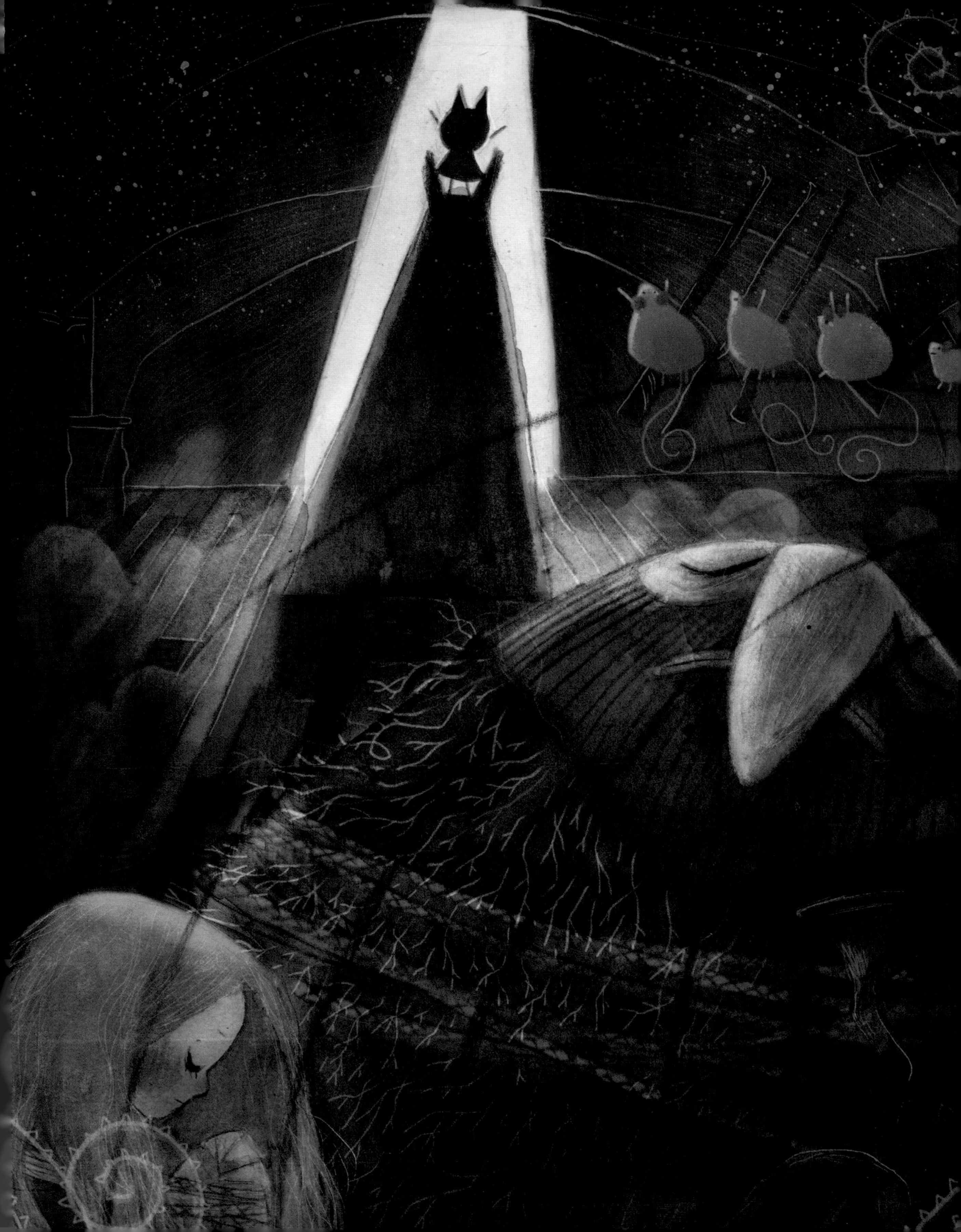

Together, the two left the gloomy
place and were happy to find the
sunny and verdant trail leading back
to their home. The little red wolf,
overjoyed, was singing and dancing
happily as he followed his dad.

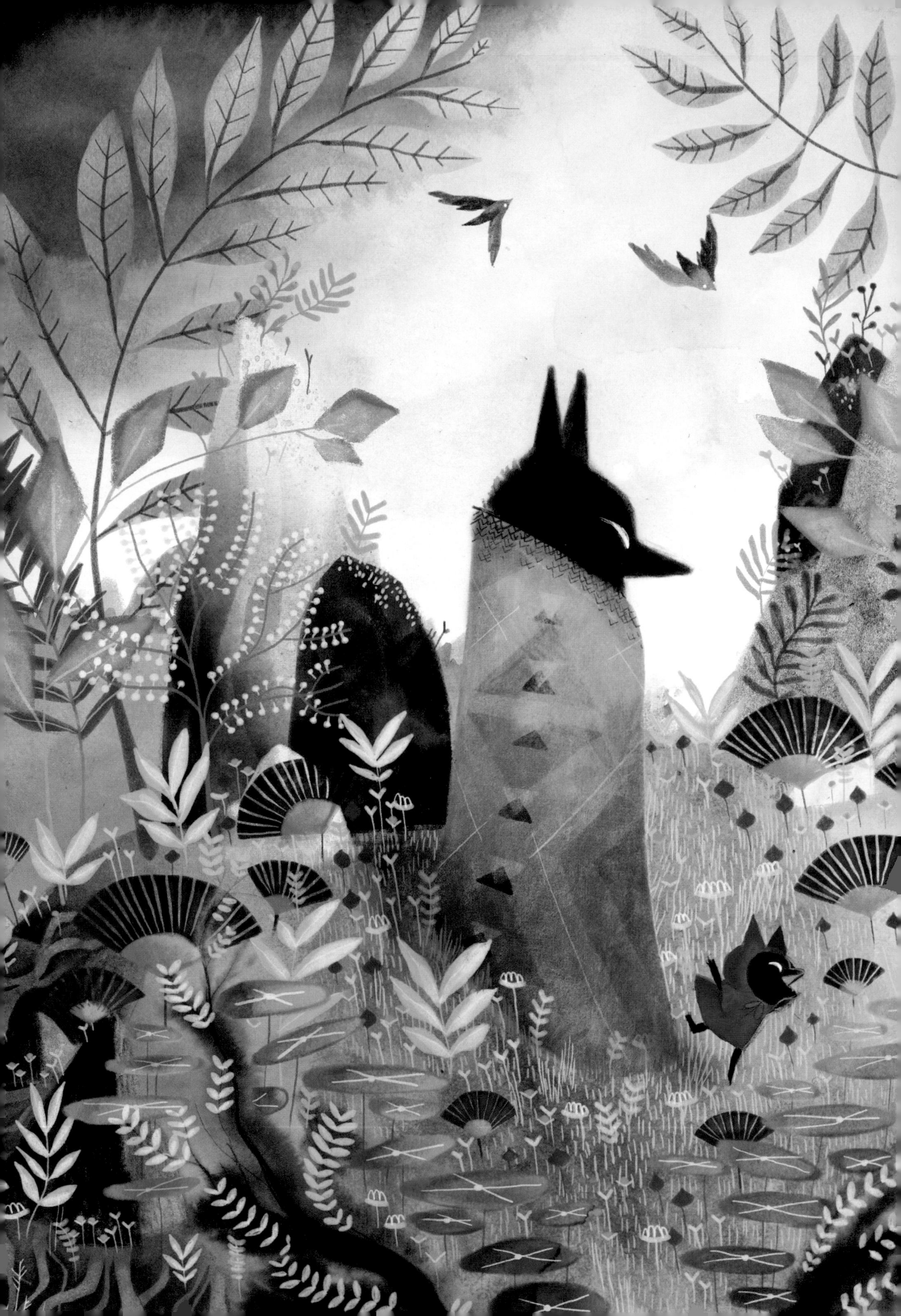

His father, surprised
by the familiar tune,
asked him:

"How do you know
that song?"

Astonished, the little
wolf realized that he
had been humming
the song of the evil
young girl, and he
told his dad the
whole story.

His dad, moved by the story,
spoke with melancholy:

"I know that song, too, but I
remember it a little differently."

And he began to sing...

"Once upon a time, there was a
strange young woman..."
"Who spent her time deep in the forest."

"The people of the village said she had no soul."

"But the village guard admired her deeply."

"And so they fell in love, and he
laid down his weapons..."

"And they lived a happy life,
deep in the trees."

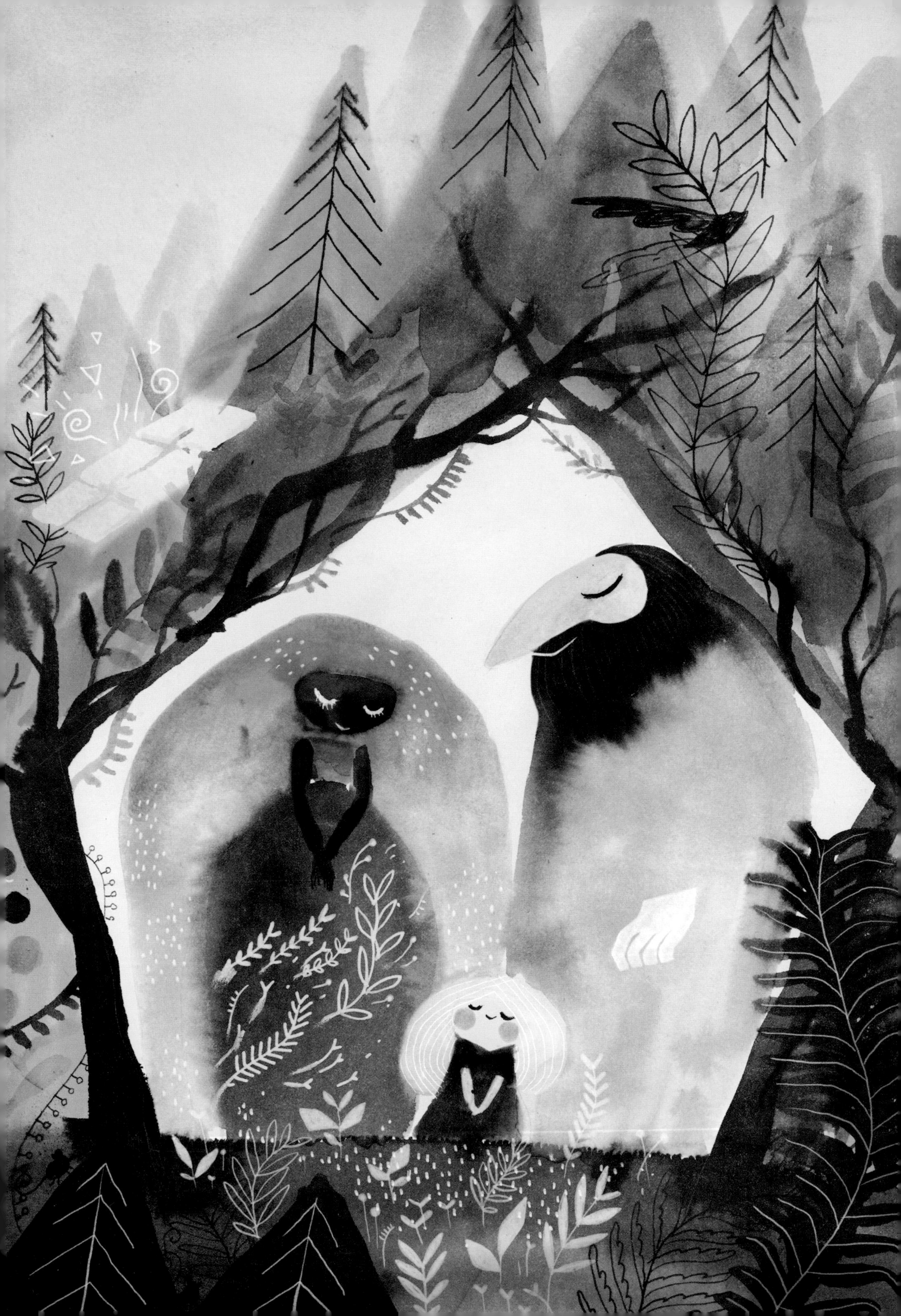

"*From dawn to dusk, she would weave magnificent capes...*"

"*And every night of the full moon she would leave her home...*"

"She would find the wolves, who truly understood her..."

"And kindly give them the precious capes she wove."

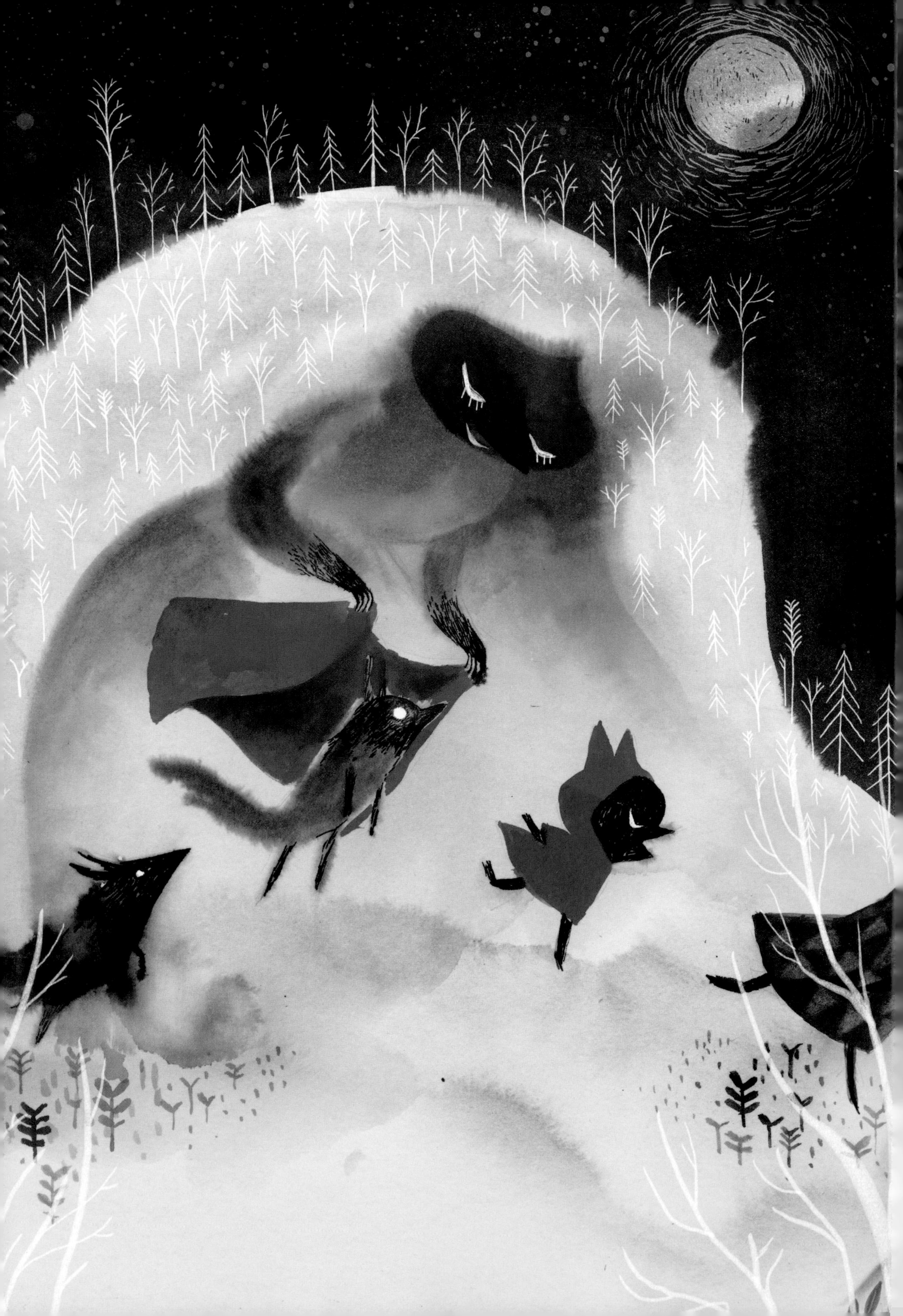

"And so began the loveliest of friendships..."
*"And under the benevolent moon, all danced
without a care in the world."*

"But one night, the hunter was
unable to find his wife..."

"*Worried, he took up his weapon
and set out to look for her.*"

"*When he found her he was blinded by fear...*"

"The man let his rifle speak, aiming only to kill."

"But in his rage, misfortune struck..."

*"So sad and horrible, that he could
never forgive himself."*

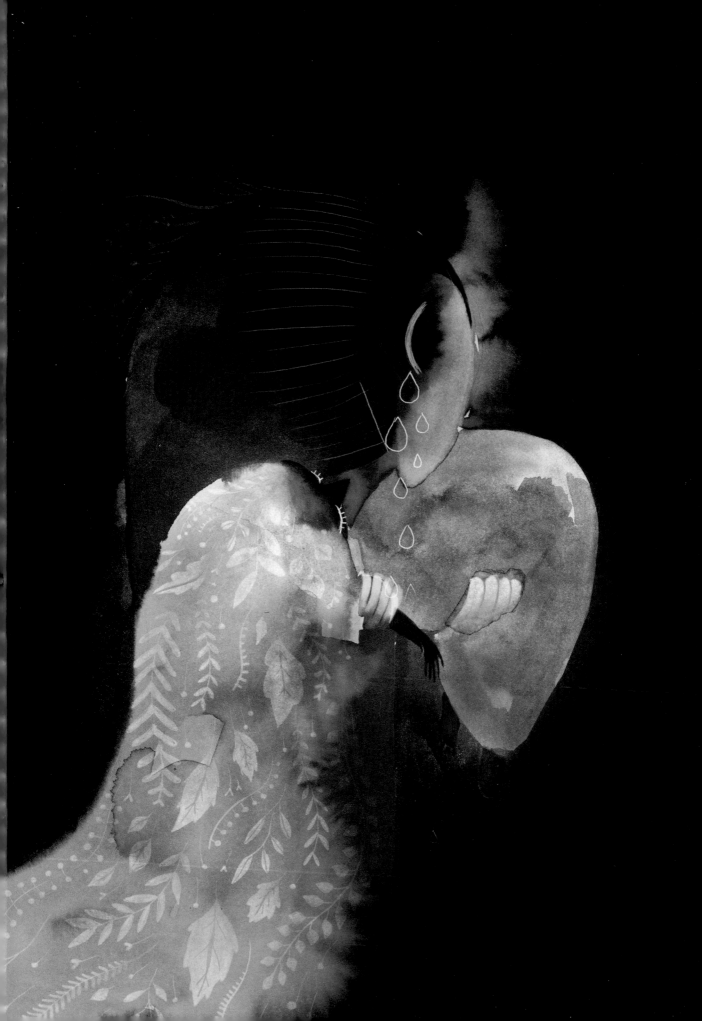

The End

English edition translated by
Jeremy Melloul

Design by
AndWorld Design

Publisher's Cataloging-In-Publication Data

(Prepared by The Donohue Group, Inc.)

Names: Fléchais, Amélie. | Perrault, Charles, 1628-1703. Petit Chaperon rouge. English. | Melloul, Jeremy, translator. | AndWorld
      Design (Firm), designer.
Title: The little red wolf / Amélie Fléchais ; English edition translated by Jeremy Melloul ; design by AndWorld Design.
Other Titles: Petit loup rouge. English
Description: English edition. | [St. Louis, Missouri] : CubHouse, 2017. | «Freely inspired by the tale Little Red Riding Hood
      by Charles Perrault»--Preliminary page. | Originally published in French under the following title: Le petit loup rouge.
      [Roubaix] : Ankama Editions, ©2014. | Summary: «Once upon a time in the middle of a thick and mysterious forest stood
      a strange tree house, the home of a little wolf known to everyone as «little red wolf»...»--Provided by publisher.
Identifiers: ISBN 978-1-941302-45-3
Subjects: LCSH: Wolves--Juvenile fiction. | Girls--Juvenile fiction. | CYAC: Wolves--Fiction. | Girls--Fiction. | LCGFT: Fairy tales. |
      Graphic novels. | GSAFD: Folklore. |
Classification: LCC PN6747.F543 P4813 2017 | DDC 843.92 398.2--dc23